THE CUPCAKE THIEF

by Ellen Jackson
illustrated by Blanche Sims

Kane Press, Inc.
New York

To Lana Haskill—E.J.

To Joanne K., Juliana H., and Ed M.,
it's always great working with you.—B.S.

Acknowledgments: Our thanks to Judge M. A. Gross, New York State Supreme Court, for helping us make this book as accurate as possible.

Library of Congress Cataloging-in-Publication Data

Jackson, Ellen B., 1943–
   The cupcake thief / by Ellen Jackson ; illustrated by Blanche Sims.
      p. cm. — (Social studies connects)
   "Civics/justice system-Grades: 1/3."
   "With fun activities!"
   Summary: When Zack accuses Tyler of stealing his cupcake, they take the matter to the school's Student Court for a trial.
   ISBN-13: 978-1-57565-247-4 (alk. paper)
   ISBN-10: 1-57565-247-1 (alk. paper)
   [1. Stealing—Fiction. 2. Courts—Fiction. 3. Schools—Fiction.] I. Sims, Blanche, ill. II. Title.
PZ7.J13247Cup 2007
   [Fic]—dc22
                              2006102070

10 9 8 7 6 5 4 3 2 1

First published in the United States of America in 2007 by Kane Press, Inc.
Printed in Hong Kong.

Social Studies Connects is a registered trademark of Kane Press, Inc.

Book Design: Edward Miller

www.kanepress.com

"WHO TOOK MY CUPCAKE?" Zack's eyes darted around the room, looking for someone to blame.

"Did you leave it at home?" asked Ms. Baker.

"Nope," said Zack. "I put it in my desk—right before we acted out Jack and the Beanstalk. And it didn't just walk off!"

"Well, I don't have it," said Brian.

"Me neither," said Marcy.

"You've heard of a nose for news?" said Erin. "Well, I've got a sniffer for sweets. Hold out your hands, everyone."

Erin sniffed her way up and down the rows. Then she pointed to—Tyler. "Ah-hah!" said Erin. "I smell chocolate!"

All through history people have had to decide who is telling the truth. It's not easy! That's one reason we have courts.

"What?" Tyler said. "Erin, you're my friend. You know I don't even *like* chocolate."

Brian reached into Tyler's desk and pulled out a cupcake with chocolate sprinkles.

"Uh-oh," said Tyler. He looked as jumpy as a flea on a hot plate.

"You . . . you cupcake-napper!" shrieked Zack.

"That's enough," said Ms. Baker. "There's only one fair way to handle this matter—Student Court. Zack and Tyler, report to Room 6 at noon."

"You're busted," Zack told Tyler. "You'll have to pick up trash on the playground. That's usually what the punishment is."

"But I'm innocent!" said Tyler.

"Yeah, sure," said Zack. "Tell it to the judge."

Courts were set up long ago to deal with crimes and to settle arguments in a fair way. In some schools, a student who breaks a rule must go to Student Court.

Just before noon, Tyler trudged toward Room 6. He looked lower than an earthworm's belly button.

"Do you mind if I tag along?" asked Erin. "Maybe I can help."

Tyler shrugged. "Anything to keep me from getting trash duty."

Tyler and Erin walked into Room 6. Zack was already there, talking to a sixth-grader named Leo.

"Hi, Tyler," said a girl with a friendly smile. "I'm Jen, your lawyer. I'll be arguing your case before the judge. What's your side of the story?"

"I . . . I don't know," said Tyler. "But I didn't take Zack's cupcake."

Jen looked deep into Tyler's eyes. "I believe you," she said.

"I'm a friend of Tyler's," said Erin. "I believe him too—and I'd like to help."

"Then you can be a witness," Jen said. "But right now I need to ask Tyler some questions."

> **DID YOU KNOW?**
> **Witnesses** tell what they have seen or know about what happened. Sometimes a witness just talks about what the person on trial is like. Each side can call witnesses.

A few minutes later, some kids sat down by a sign that said Jury.

The judge banged his gavel. "The court will come to order," he said. "Tyler, you are accused of taking Zack's cupcake. Zack and his lawyer, Leo, will tell Zack's side of the story. Then you will have your turn. The jury will decide if you're guilty."

STUDENT COURT
WHERE THE TRUTH RULES
Today's Cases:
1) Did Sam Skol put paint in Linda Gee's hair?
2) Did Tyler Grey steal Zack Dalin's cupcake?
3) Did Jake Ryan put yogurt in Room 4's pencil sharpener?

DID YOU KNOW?
The **judge** makes sure that a trial is fair and that the law is followed.

Tyler looked sadder than a bowl of wilted spinach.

"Zack's lawyer will now call the first witness," said the judge.

JURORS
Don't make up your minds until you hear all the facts!

REMEMBER
Be totally sure before you say someone is guilty!

JURY

DID YOU KNOW?
A **jury** decides whether someone has done what he or she is accused of doing. A person who is on a jury is called a **juror**. Every juror must promise to be fair.

"I call Zack," said Leo.

"Raise your right hand," the judge told Zack. "Do you promise to tell the whole truth?"

"Yup," Zack said. He parked himself in the witness seat and faced the jury.

"When did you first notice that your cupcake was missing?" asked Leo.

"Just before noon," said Zack. "I reached into my desk, and it was gone."

Zack told the jury how Erin had helped find the cupcake. Then he pointed right at Tyler. "He took my cupcake and hid it in his desk. Look at those shifty eyes. Doesn't he look like a criminal?"

The jury nodded as if they agreed.

"I object!" said Jen. "That's not fair."

The judge frowned. "Stick to the facts, Zack."

Then it was Jen's turn to question Zack. "Did you *see* Tyler take the cupcake?" she asked.

"Well, no," said Zack.

"And you got it back, didn't you?" she asked.

Zack made a face. "Yes. But it had finger marks on it. Who wants a used cupcake? It probably had cooties."

Truth or Trouble!
The lawyers on both sides have a chance to ask the witnesses about what happened. Each witness must promise to tell the truth. Witnesses who lie can end up in jail!

"May we see this cupcake?" Jen asked Zack.

"I . . . I . . . ate it," he said.

The jury gasped.

"You *ate* the evidence?" asked the judge.

"I thought you didn't want a used cupcake."

Zack shrugged. "I was hungry."

"*Sheesh!*" muttered a juror.

"Do you have any more questions for Zack?" asked the judge. Jen shook her head.

"Our side rests," said Leo. "That means it's Jen's turn to give evidence."

"I know that," said Jen. "I call Erin."

Erin promised to tell the truth and sat down.

"I've known Tyler since kindergarten," she said. "He's never stolen anything, and I don't believe he took the cupcake. Tyler doesn't even like sweets! Last Halloween he gave away all his candy."

Jen smiled. "Your turn," she said to Leo.

"No questions," Leo grumbled. "It's clear that Erin thinks Tyler is a great guy."

"I call Tyler," said Jen.

Tyler said he'd tell the truth and took a seat.
His face was as long as a snake's suspenders.

"Tyler," said Jen. "Did you bring your lunch to
school today?"

"Yes," said Tyler. "I brought a tuna sandwich. But I ate it at morning recess. I was hungry."

Zack stood up. "Sounds *fishy* to me." He laughed at his own joke. "Har, har, har!"

"Order in the court!" said the judge.

19

"Tyler, would you mind letting the jury smell your breath?" asked Jen.

"Ugh!" said one of the jurors.

Tyler walked to the roped-off area and opened his mouth.

"That's tuna fish, all right," said another juror. "You smell just like my cat."

"Do you have any questions for Tyler?" Jen
asked Leo.

"Just one," Leo said. "Why tuna? You look
like a peanut-butter-and-jelly kid to me."

Jen rolled her eyes. "I call—Zack."

Zack plopped down and waved to the jury.

"How big was your cupcake, Zack?" asked Jen.

"Gynormous," said Zack with a smile.

"And how big is Tyler?" asked Jen.

"About the size of pond scum." Zack smirked. "He's the smallest kid in the class."

"I see," said Jen. "Not the kind of kid to want a gynormous cupcake after eating a tuna sandwich?"

Zack shrugged.

"I have another question," Jen continued. "What was the class doing right before you noticed your cupcake was missing?"

"A math lesson," said Zack. "I think."

"And before that?" asked Jen.

Zack looked as confused as a baby learning algebra.

"Omigosh!" Erin jumped up and waved her arms. "Tyler didn't do it!" she yelled. "He's innocent!"

Everyone began talking at once.

"Order! Order in the court!" said the judge.

"But I just remembered!" said Erin. "Right after recess, the class acted out Jack and the Beanstalk. Zack played the Giant, and Tyler was the Goose That Lays Golden Eggs. We pushed all the desks to the side of the room, and—"

"Erin's right!" shouted Tyler. He turned to the judge. "Can the jury visit the scene of the crime?"

Everybody followed Tyler to Room 3.
"We were laughing so hard after the play," Tyler said, "I think we each grabbed the wrong desk. I took Zack's, and he took mine. It was one big mistake."

Tyler reached inside the desk he'd been sitting at. He pulled out a comic book, a banana peel, and a dirty sock. "Look, Zack," he said. "Isn't that your sock? It's too big for me."

"And here's my stink bug," said Zack. "I wondered where it went."

"But Tyler, why did I smell chocolate on your
fingers?" asked Erin.

"When I reached in the desk for my math book,
I must have touched some sprinkles," he said.

"Yep, there's one under your nail," said Erin.

The jury whispered together in the corner.
Then one juror said in a loud voice, "We find
Tyler—not guilty."

"Case dismissed," said the judge.

Courts do their best to
be fair. Do you think
Tyler had a fair trial?
Why or why not?

"Well, that's that," Zack said to Tyler. "Too bad about the little mix-up."

"Zack!" said Ms. Baker. "Did you bring another stink bug to school? That's the third time this month." She crossed her arms.

"Uh-oh," said Zack. "I think I'm busted. . . ."

And he was.

MAKING CONNECTIONS

Suppose your school was a "rule-free zone." Think about it. Anyone could steal your lunch, take your markers without asking, or put a stink bomb in your locker! Hmm, on second thought, maybe a "rule-free zone" wouldn't be such a good idea after all. . . .

In some schools, kids help write the rules and decide what happens if they're broken. When you follow the rules, you show respect for them. Rules and laws are a lot alike. They make life better for everyone!

Look Back
- On page 6, what does Tyler say? Where is he going on page 7? How does going there show he respects the school rules?
- On pages 12, 16, and 18, what do Zack, Erin, and Tyler promise to do? Explain why it's important to respect this rule.
- Read page 30. Why is Ms. Baker angry? What does she say that shows Zack knew the rule?

Try This!
These three kids are breaking rules. Choose a fair punishment for each kid.